ONE LITTLE MONSTER

ALADDIN
An imprint of Simon & Schuster
Children's Publishing Division •
1230 Avenue of the Americas, New York,
New York 10020 • First Aladdin hardcover edition
July 2018 • Copyright © 2018 by Mark Gonyea • All
rights reserved, including the right of reproduction in
whole or in part in any form. • ALADDIN and related logo
are registered trademarks of Simon & Schuster, Inc. • For
information about special discounts for bulk purchases, please
contact Simon & Schuster Special Sales at 1-866-506-1949
or business@simonandschuster.com. • The Simon & Schuster
Speakers Bureau can bring authors to your live event. For more
information or to book an event contact the Simon & Schuster
Speakers Bureau at 1-866-248-3049 or visit our website at
www.simonspeakers.com. • Book designed by Mark Gonyea
& Laura Lyn DiSiena • The illustrations for this book were
rendered digitally. • The text of this book was set in
Big Simple. • Manufactured in China 0518 SCP •
1 2 3 4 5 6 7 8 9 10 • Library of Congress
Control Number 2017955456 •
ISBN 978-1-5344-0674-2 (hc) •
ISBN 978-1-5344-0675-9 (eBook)

ONE LITTLE MONSTER

WRITTEN AND
ILLUSTRATED BY
MARK GONYEA

ALADDIN

New York London Toronto Sydney New Delhi

I'M COZY IN BED, AND WHAT DO I SEE?

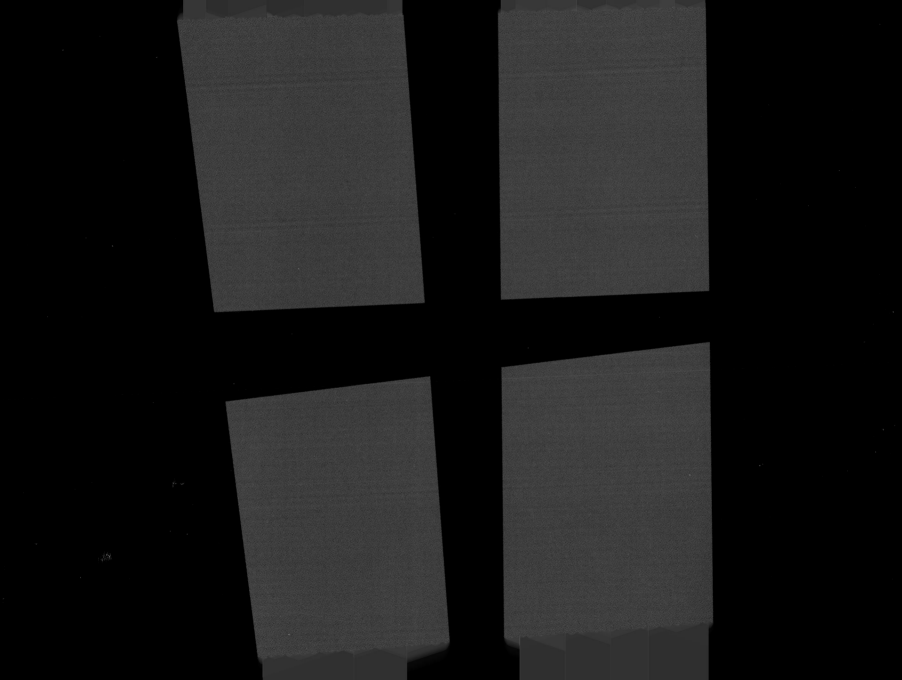

1 LITTLE MONSTER STARING AT ME.

I SAY TO MYSELF,
WHAT HARM COULD IT DO?

I ONLY BLINKED ONCE . . .

BUT NOW I SEE 2!

2 LITTLE MONSTERS.
ARE THEY SEARCHING FOR ME?

ONE HAS
A BIG SNEEZE.

3 LITTLE MONSTERS ARE NOW ON THE FLOOR.

ONE WAS IN HIDING.

THE COUNT IS NOW 4.

4 LITTLE MONSTERS.
ONE CUTS THE CHEESE.

NOW I SMELL 5!
HOLD YOUR NOSE,
PLEASE.

5 LITTLE MONSTERS
MAKE ANOTHER FROM BRICKS!

ALL DANCING AROUND.
IT'S A PARTY OF 6.

6 LITTLE MONSTERS SHUDDER AND SHAKE.
ONE SLIPS ON SOME OOZE.

INTO **7** THEY BREAK.

7 LITTLE MONSTERS SERVE
UP A SURPRISE.
BUT THEY CAN'T FOOL ME.

It's number 8 in disguise!

8 LITTLE MONSTERS FOLLOW MY SIGN.

MONSTER PARTY! THIS WAY! ➡

OUT POPS ANOTHER . . .

THIS
END
UP ▶

MAIL TO:.
FAR AWAY

DO NOT
OPEN

MAIL TO:
FAR AWAY

DO NOT
OPEN

THIS
END
UP ◀

RIGHT AFTER MY NAP.